PUFFIN BOOKS

The Good and Bad Witch

Chris Nicholls has spent most of his working life in English teaching of one sort or another, while trying to write when work allowed. He then became freelance on the two fronts of writing for children and teaching English as a foreign language. *The Good and Bad Witch* is his fifth book to be published. He has six children and lives in Shropshire.

Another book by Chris Nicholls

The Good and Bad Witch at School

CHRIS NICHOLLS

The *Good* and **Bad** Witch

Illustrated by Toni Goffe

PUFFIN BOOKS

For Kathy, who always liked witches

PUFFIN BOOKS

Published by the Penguin Group
Penguin Books Ltd, 27 Wrights Lane, London W8 5TZ, England
Penguin Books USA Inc., 375 Hudson Street, New York, New York 10014, USA
Penguin Books Australia Ltd, Ringwood, Victoria, Australia
Penguin Books Canada Ltd, 10 Alcorn Avenue, Toronto, Ontario, Canada M4V 3B2
Penguin Books (NZ) Ltd, 182–190 Wairau Road, Auckland 10, New Zealand

Penguin Books Ltd, Registered Offices: Harmondsworth, Middlesex, England

First published by Hamish Hamilton 1994
Published in Puffin Books 1996
10 9 8 7 6 5 4 3 2 1

Text copyright © Chris Nicholls, 1994
Illustrations copyright © Toni Goffe, 1994
All rights reserved

The moral right of the author has been asserted

Filmset in Baskerville

Made and printed in England by Clays Ltd, St Ives plc

Chapter 1
Good and Bad in Mr Squirmage's Store

VIRBENA HARPY WAS a good and bad witch. That doesn't mean that sometimes her spells worked and sometimes they didn't. It means that she was like you and me, only a bit more so – sometimes sweet, kind and lovable; sometimes mean, nasty and all the hateful things we can't help being just a bit, very occasionally.

The trouble was that being a witch the things she could do with her magic when she was bad were truly horrible. On the other hand the things she could do with her magic when she was good

1

were often wonderful and made people happy and smiling for miles around.

Being a witch she had to have a cat, of course. But being a good and bad witch she had to have two cats – one Good, one Bad. Malic was her Bad cat – a big, spitting, scratching she-cat, dark grey, with ferocious green eyes and a tail like a lashing whip.

Her Good cat was called Amy, a warm, orange cat with silky-thick fur and gentle, yellowy eyes which closed so peacefully when you stroked her, while a purring went up as loud and lovely as a birthday party.

One more thing you should know about Virbena Harpy is that her Bad times came and went so quickly that quite often they caught her by surprise, like a sudden thunderstorm. Sometimes they were set off by

2

something unpleasant happening; sometimes they just came. She never quite knew what to expect from herself.

Like, for instance, the time she went to buy some powdered birchbark from the WITCHES GENERAL SUPPLY STORE in Hallowington.

Mr Squirmage, the storekeeper, was used to dealing with witches because that was his job. He was also used to dealing with witches who turned nasty when he hadn't got the supplies they needed for their spells. He'd been changed into frogs, worms, mice and beetles more times than he could remember. Once, even, three witches had turned on him at the same time and he'd ended up as a sort of furry water-snake with little horns.

But naturally Mr Squirmage kept his own book of spells in the shop, as well as all the ingredients he could possibly need, so as soon as the angry customer had left he would just crawl,

4

creep or hop over to the book, find the right anti-spell, and make himself a mixture which changed him back into his usual self in a twinkling.

Making mixtures when you've only got wings or flippers or fins, or even nothing but a small mouth to hold the spoon with, isn't easy, though, and he

did not like being changed into things. This made him rather too keen to please – a bit over-anxious. In a word, slimy.

"Ah, good afternoon, madam," he said, as soon as Virbena came into the store. "And what can I do for madam today, thank you and please, madam?"

At this moment Virbena was decidedly in a Good mood. She wanted the powdered birchbark to help a fierce old lady called Mrs Gunderblast to get rid of a large spot which had appeared on the end of her nose. So, in spite of the fact that she couldn't stand the storekeeper's slimy manner, she answered him pleasantly enough.

"Half a pound of best powdered birchbark, please, Mr Squirmage, and what a lovely day it is today."

"Indeed it is, it is, it is, madam," Mr Squirmage replied, going over to the shelf where he kept the powdered barks, adding, "and yesterday was very lovely too, and so was tomorrow also, madam, I don't doubt."

Now, in fact, yesterday it had been hailing and thundering most of the day, and when it hadn't been, there'd been an east wind sharp as a kitchen knife. Virbena began to feel a tiny bit irritated, but she quickly got a grip on herself because she knew what could happen if she didn't.

Mr Squirmage came back with a large jar of powder. He began to tip some into the pan of the scales on the counter.

"Excuse me one moment, Mr Squirmage," Virbena said most politely. "I hope you don't mind my asking, but are you sure that pan is quite clean?"

She asked this because she knew that unspeakable things could happen if even the slightest trace of the wrong sort of stuff got mixed in by accident. For example, the merest speck of borage root in the spell for Mrs Gunderblast's spot would turn her nose into a toffee-apple, which would be terrible because her tongue was certainly not long enough to reach up and lick it.

"Clean, madam? Why yes, it is absolutely most very clean, madam. All my equipment is always kept shiningly spotless at each and every time, madam."

But Virbena knew. She had sharp eyes, and she had seen *something* – she wasn't sure what – lurking in the bottom of the scales pan before Mr Squirmage had covered it with the powder. Once again she felt herself growing angry, and once again she calmed herself.

Then her eyes fell suddenly on the label of the jar that Mr Squirmage was pouring from. The label did not say "POWDERED BIRCHBARK". It said "POWDERED BITCH-BARK".

Now as you may know, a *birch* is a sort of tree with shining silver bark, but *bitch* is the word for a lady dog, and bitches bark much less than men dogs, who bark at anything and everybody. So BITCH-BARK powder is not easy to come by, and is used only for the most expensive kinds of spells, such as turning bubblegum into Christmas trees.

What powdered BITCH-BARK would have done to the spot on Mrs Gunderblast's nose, Virbena could not begin to imagine. In any case, she didn't have time to try, because she was beginning to go . . . BAD.

It could be quite exciting to watch Virbena Harpy turning Bad, as long as you were completely certain you were not going to be at the receiving end. Mr Squirmage didn't find it exciting; he found it terrifying.

First her cheeks go a little red, then all at once the red rushes up to the rims of her eyes, while the rest of her face turns green – pale then dark. Her hair starts to curl up into tight knots, but suddenly shoots stiffly out like hundreds of sharp sticks, so that if she's wearing a hat it gets jerked violently up above her head, balanced on top.

Most terrifying of all, her eyes burn like dark coals in a red-hot grate. On bad Bad days a little smoke escapes from her nose and mouth, and her soft and gentle hands change into fearsome leathery claws.

"M-m-m-m-my m-m-mistake, m-madam," stuttered poor Mr Squirmage.

It was too late. Virbena was beginning to growl out a spell:

> *Mumble-jumble,*
> *Garbage crumble –*

pointing the middle finger of her left hand straight at Mr Squirmage's belly. She was so angry she didn't know exactly what she was doing. She wanted to turn Mr Squirmage into something so confusing that it would take him days to go through his different bits of scales and tails, of jaws and paws, working himself back into something like a human being.

But halfway through the spell, she suddenly changed her mind, and the middle finger of her left hand began to swing wildly about, pointing all over the store – at this shelf, then that; at the locked cupboards of poisons; at the stacked tins of muck and root-rot; at the freezers packed with all kinds of frozen slime.

And as she pointed and continued to
growl, she began to stamp a
dance-rhythm with her left foot:

Mix-up, muddle-up,
Jig-about and fuddle-up –

Then the tins and jars and packets
began dancing about in time, till with
a great chorus of crashes their lids
burst off and the air was filled with
flying nastiness. Powders and potions,
liquids and lozenges, zoomed here and
there looking for new homes. It was

like Musical Jars. A cloud of bat-droppings roared three times round the light, then dived into an empty slug-slime packet. A huge bunch of giant hogweed was trying madly to thrust itself into a tiny jar labelled ESSENCE OF SLUDGE.

At first Mr Squirmage didn't realise what was happening. When he did realise he wasn't much happier.

"Oh, p-please," he whimpered – but he might as well have tried to stop a steamroller with a jelly-baby.

Eventually things did quieten down. The last gob of slime plopped into a sack that had once held Wart Mixture. The giant hogweed gave up and flopped sulkily onto the floor. Even the hair on Virbena's head was beginning to un-stiffen, and her hat to lower itself a little.

"There, Mr Squirmage," she cackled. "I guess *that* will teach you to get things muddled up. Good day to you."

And she sailed out of the shop without her feet touching the floor once.

Well, it may have been one thing for Virbena Harpy to take her anger out on Mr Squirmage but it was quite another what she'd done to the many witches and wizards who used his store. Mr Squirmage made a huge effort to get things back in their right places, but meanwhile there were customers – often very impatient customers – clamouring to buy things for delicate spells.

So there were mistakes – lots of mistakes. One wizard came in to buy a jar of cuckoo-spit for a spell that would

fly him to the moon. He was given a
jar which said CUCKOO-SPIT on it,
but which actually contained
MOLE-SPIT. So instead of flying up,
up to the moon he found himself
burrowing down, down into the
ground, till he came out in Australia
and had to come home by plane.

Finally they could stand it no longer,
and they all came in a gang to
Virbena's house one tea-time and sat
there complaining at her while they
drank her lemon tea and ate up all her
chocolate cake.

Virbena was feeling quite Good
again by this time, but the trouble was
that when she was Good, she couldn't
always remember exactly what she'd
done when she was Bad. She was
horrified when they told her.

"I didn't, did I?" she said, a huge

frown clouding her pretty face. "I'm so sorry."

"'Sorry' isn't good enough, Virbena Harpy," screeched a nasty old witch called Dulwich, who had only one ear, and that not a very nice one. "I put a curse of cockroaches on my next-door neighbour, and what did he get? Diamonds! He's one of the richest men in the world now. No, 'sorry' just isn't good enough."

"You'll have to put it right," said a wizened young wizard. "And soon."

So put it right she had to. It's not so difficult saying a spell to muddle things up, but putting them straight is much less easy. In fact after trying one spell which simply turned several of the jars into black kittens, Virbena had to do it all by hand – which meant working for three weeks in Mr Squirmage's store,

carrying stuff backwards and forwards, washing out jars and bottles, and repacking.

And did Mr Squirmage once say "Thank you" to her? Well, actually he did, but not just once – once a minute, more like. And when he didn't say "Thank you", he said "Thank you *very* very much – thank you *so* much."

By the end of it all, Virbena was so screamingly fed up with his creepiness, so worn out with work, so near breaking point, that she was ready to go Bad with just about anyone who did the tiniest thing wrong.

And that is almost exactly what happened, as you'll see . . .

Chapter 2
Help!

IT MAY SURPRISE you to hear that as well as her two cats Virbena had a very normal sort of family. She had a good-tempered, down-to-earth husband called Bill, who drove a taxi and who thought all magic was nonsense. They had two children – a girl called Lorna, and a boy called James, two years older. And they all lived together in a sweet black-and-white cottage in the village of Charmers.

Lorna was a lively child, thin and wiry, always on the move, fidgety. James was big, solid, and liked being the boss. Neither of *them* thought magic was nonsense: they thought it was like electricity – useful but very dangerous. James hoped desperately that Virbena might one day consider him old enough to begin learning about it, but Lorna preferred poking her nose into other things.

You might wonder whether Virbena ever turned Bad with them, because even the nicest of mums have been known to get cross when toys are left on the stairs for people to trip headlong over, or the bathroom floor is suddenly awash with soapsuds and plastic ducks.

And of course the answer is, yes, she did turn Bad with them occasionally, but never seriously Bad – except for just once maybe.

It was the very day after she'd

finished the awful job of straightening
out the mess she'd made in Mr
Squirmage's store. She'd gradually
got so tired and so irritated that finally
she felt almost ill and she simply had
to go upstairs to rest for a short
while.

The moment she'd gone out of the
room James suddenly had the nice idea
of suggesting to Lorna that they should
try and help their mother by doing
some of her jobs. Lorna agreed because
she too was a kind, helpful child – and
also because it might mean a chance of
messing with things she wasn't usually
allowed to touch.

There were two main jobs to be
done first, James decided – hoovering
the living-room and washing up the
breakfast things. Lorna immediately
shouted, "I bags hoovering!"

This was because Virbena had never let her near the vacuum-cleaner ever since the time Lorna had got fascinated by trying to see how big its sucking power actually was, and had gone round letting it suck up anything the tube would take – coins, Virbena's sewing things, all the sugar out of a big bagful, sweets, socks, and much more besides.

Having forgotten this, James obediently went and fetched the cleaner for Lorna, plugged it in and switched it on. But then, just as he was about to hand her the sucking end of the tube he did remember and yelled, "No, you're not allowed to do this. You do the washing-up."

Not surprisingly, Lorna was a bit upset by having her job snatched away from her at the last moment, so *she*

snatched – at the tube – yelling, "No,
I'm doing this!"

What happened next was sudden
and astonishing because Lorna's grab
not only pulled the tube right off the
main part of the cleaner but also rolled
it over on its back, and this must have
accidentally flicked the switch from
suck to blow.

First a few lumps of carpet fluff shot

25

out, followed then by a great volcano of dust, bursting out and up, filling the air so thick that James and Lorna knew they'd begin to cough themselves silly if they stayed in the room a moment longer. Quickly switching the cleaner off, James seized Lorna's hand and they raced out into the hall, out through the front door, gulping in the fresh air.

They started their quarrel out there while the dust was settling inside: the usual sort of quarrel – "Your fault!" "Wasn't!" "You shouldn't have . . ." "Yes, I should, and anyway *you* shouldn't have . . ." And so on.

Then they came in, still shouting at each other through the hall, to inspect the damage in the living-room. It was bad – thick dust over everything and a great pile of muck just in front of the cleaner. It was so bad that it shut them up for five seconds before they started off accusing each other again.

Suddenly they became aware of something, and their voices died feebly away. Virbena, in the doorway, taking the whole scene in.

She went Bad very quickly – so quickly that James and Lorna had time to take only two frightened steps backwards before their dear mother was standing in front of them as a full-blown, green and smoking witch.

She didn't say much. In fact she didn't say anything the children could understand. She just did some very fancy hand-waving over them as they cowered there, muttered three strange phrases, then turned and swept out of the room. They heard her bedroom door slam shut.

It was a few seconds before James or Lorna dared to move. Then they turned to look at each other. The room, the furniture, the lumps of carpet fluff all seemed very big. What was even odder, James couldn't see Lorna at all, and Lorna couldn't see

James. Each saw only a small green frog, squatting in the dust.

James took a step forward to see if Lorna had gone out of the room without him noticing, but suddenly found himself sailing up into the air. He landed with a little plop a short distance ahead of where he'd been. Next moment there was another plop, and the other frog landed beside him. Only then did they both understand what had happened.

The two frogs stared at each other. James-frog opened his mouth to say, "She's turned us into frogs," but all that came out were tiny croaking noises. The other frog – the Lorna-frog – was making croaking noises too, but he had no idea what they meant.

The obvious thing to do, James-frog thought, was for them to hop up the

stairs and hang about outside
Virbena's door, hoping that she'd
come out in a good enough mood to
change them back again. He started off
towards the sitting-room door, looking
round each time he landed to see that
Lorna-frog was following him. It was
really quite a nice way of moving
about, he decided. Hop – sail – plop,
Hop – sail – plop.

It was when they got out into the
hallway, and were just about to go up
the stairs, that James-frog noticed the
front door was still open. And as he
did so a terrible feeling came over his
skin. It felt so itchy, so hard and dry.
It had to have something on it
urgently.

Water! That was it. He had to find
water, *now*.

It was such a hugely strong feeling

that he forgot all about Lorna and, instead of going to the stairs, hopped madly for the open front door.

He knew where he was making for, and luckily it wasn't too far – a little ornamental pond which Mum and Dad had finished making a few months ago, which Dad said was for nice plants like water-lilies and Mum said was for 'useful' plants.

James hopped and hopped, his skin feeling worse all the time, off the front doorstep, onto the path, off the path onto the lawn. He could see the stones round the pond, nearer – hop – nearer, till, with a last frantic leap he was there. He didn't stop to think about the way frogs swim but dived straight in.

It was delicious; like being horribly thirsty then suddenly getting a long,

cool drink. And even before he'd got
over the thrill of that, there were other
pleasures crowding in; how beautifully
quick and easy swimming felt; how
well your eyes could see underwater;
how you could stay down for ages
without popping up for air.

Round and round the pond he swam, delighting in the powerful thrusts of his back legs and how far each thrust took him. It was the most exciting thing he'd ever done.

Gradually, though, he began to sense something disturbing the water ahead. A prickly feeling which said 'DANGER!' came over him, and he began to swim more slowly. He knew that no one had put any fish into the pond yet, just a few boring water-lilies.

It seemed safer to climb out, and James swam to the edge till he found a gap between two stones where he could crawl up onto the side.

Looking back he could see nothing in the water except for the water-lily pads out in the middle, but then his eye was caught by something crawling out on the far side of the pond –

another frog doing exactly what he'd done. It must surely be Lorna.

Almost at the same moment he felt a movement behind him. Turning, he saw just one hop away an evil, dark grey face about three times as big as himself, slanting green eyes with black slits. Malic the Bad cat!

He heard a warning, screaming croak from across the pond as he gave the most gigantic hop out – splash! into the safety of the water. Then once again he was swimming round, but this time in panic. He'd watched Malic 'fishing' before – dipping her paws in the water to hoick out anything that moved. He swam underwater towards the middle, only to see new dangers – dark round shapes above him.

But then he realised. They were water-lily pads of course. Frogs often

sat on those, and there was no danger
of Malic swimming out to them. He
surfaced, and crawled up onto the
nearest pad.

Malic was on the edge of the pond,
standing staring angrily over at him,
tail lashing violently. And Lorna?

A pair of skinny arms came up over the edge of the pad next to him, followed by a wide mouth and a pair of bulging eyes. And then there they were, two little green frogs next to each other on two dark green lily pads, while two fierce green eyes glared at them from across the water.

The problem was what to do now. Malic had sat down, with the tip of her tail twitching and James knew that she was quite capable of sitting there for hours. In which case how could they ever get across safely to their mother to be changed back?

And then to their joy, they saw Virbena coming out of the front door towards them, no longer green and smoking but her usual, dear self. James and Lorna looked at each other, and each wondered if the other was smiling. It isn't easy to know if a frog's smiling, even if you're a frog yourself.

Virbena came to the edge of the pond and stood for a moment gazing over at her two little child-frogs. Then she bent down and scooped Malic up in her arms. And of course immediately the child-frogs saw that, they dived straight off their lily pads and swam towards her.

I don't know whether it was because Virbena decided that the children had got off too lightly or whether she simply made a mistake. Anyway, one moment James and Lorna were enjoying their last smooth glide through the water, and the next moment they were on their hands and knees in the shallows at the edge of the pond, spluttering, soaked to the skin, hair dripping into their eyes.

"Mum!" they both wailed together,
and James said, "You could have
waited till we'd got out, couldn't you?"

"Oh, I'm so, *so* sorry," Virbena
gushed (but with just a hint of a
pleased smile). "What a silly mistake!
You'll just have to run and get
changed at once."

"But then," she shouted as they
began to drip their way across the
lawn, "I think you've both got a little
housework to do, haven't you?"

39

Chapter 3
In Which Nearly
Everyone Gets Ratty

VIRBENA AND HER family hadn't
always lived in their delightful cottage
in Charmers. At one time, before Bill
Harpy had saved up enough money to
buy his own taxi, they lived on the
fourteenth floor of a huge block of flats
in the city of Grimsbury.

Witches are not nearly so common
in big cities. People there are not used
to them and don't like them. They
have to keep their magic very secret,
and that was sometimes extremely
difficult for Virbena, because people
can be very annoying and rude in cities

– like the time she lost her bus ticket when she was coming back from the swimming baths with James and Lorna one afternoon.

All she did was to drop it on the floor by mistake when she was getting her handkerchief out. She didn't drop the children's tickets, just her own. And that wouldn't have mattered too much, only before she noticed it had gone, someone else must have picked it up to use for themselves.

Even that wouldn't have mattered if an Inspector hadn't got on the bus at the very next stop to check tickets. He happened to be one of those rather stupid people who don't listen, don't understand when they do listen, and don't want to help when they do understand.

"If you haven't got a ticket, you'll

have to buy another," he said to her sharply.

"But I'm afraid I haven't got any more money on me," said Virbena, smiling her best possible smile at him in the hope that he might really be nicer than he looked.

But he wasn't. He just glared at Virbena and said, "In that case you'll have to get off the bus and walk, won't you?"

"But my children can't walk that far."

"You should have thought of that before you spent all your money."

"I did think of it! Look, my children have got tickets – I wouldn't have bought them tickets and not myself one, would I?"

"If your children have tickets, they can of course stay on the bus."

"They're far too young to stay on alone without their mother. Anyway, I'm sure the driver can remember I got a ticket for myself too."

The Inspector went and had a word with the driver, then came back.

"The driver says there are far too many passengers for him to remember whether each one's got a ticket."

All this time, Virbena had been struggling like made not to lose her temper. She patiently collected all the swimming bags together ready to get off the bus and face the long walk home with two very tired children. Then the Inspector made it impossible. He chose to add heavily, "And don't try that trick again, will you madam, or you'll be in serious trouble."

That did it. Virbena *was* in serious trouble, but not the kind the Inspector meant. She was turning . . . Bad!

Even though they were younger then, James and Lorna had already seen it happen before so they weren't too frightened. She was their own mum, after all. But the Inspector *was* frightened – very. His uniform suddenly seemed several sizes too big for him as he shrank inside it, and little whimpering noises came out of its neck-hole.

"I d-d-didn't mean . . ."

Then there was no Inspector. Only a smallish rat with pink eyes, wiry tail and a twitching snout, sitting among the litter of tickets on the floor of the bus. It gazed helplessly up at Virbena, squeaking.

Of course even before that happened – in fact the moment Virbena began to change – everyone on the bus had turned to see what was going on. James and Lorna never forgot the feeling of sitting there, one each side of their weird mother, with that sea of shocked and angry faces all around, staring.

"Hey, that isn't right," said an elderly grey-haired man in a dark suit, pointing at the rat on the floor. "You're a witch, you are."

"Didn't ought to be allowed," a thin-faced woman chimed in. She already looked as much like a rat as she could without actually being one.

And maybe that was what gave Virbena the idea that if they were going to make a fuss, they might as well *all* be rats. So she swooped both

47

her arms around, muttered some
words, and suddenly they were – all
except James, Lorna, herself and the
driver. Every seat that had held a
passenger now held a squeaking rat.
The noise was deafening.

It was lucky that the bus didn't have a nasty accident, because naturally when the driver turned round to see what the row was, he was surprised enough to stay turned round longer than was safe, and only a blaring hoot from a lorry he just missed turned him to the front again. He quickly pulled the bus in to the side of the street and stopped it.

"Drive on!" Virbena screeched at him. "This isn't a bus stop!"

The driver didn't answer. He sat with his head buried in his hands as if he was hoping that all this was some silly dream.

Virbena when Bad was not a patient witch. She shrieked, "Get a move on!" once more. But the driver either couldn't or wouldn't. Next moment there was one more rat.

Now James and Lorna were beginning to wonder how they were going to get home, but they were much too sensible to say anything at all. And clearly the same worry was crossing Virbena's mind, because she sat there mumbling and cursing, with little puffs of smoke coming out of her ears, for a few moments. Then she gathered the swimming bags in her claw-like hands again, screeched, "Come on, you pair!" at James and Lorna, and led them off the bus.

People did stare rather as they set off for home. Strange-looking folk with purple or orange hair were quite common in Grimsbury, but they were quite ordinary really, compared with Virbena Harpy when she was Bad.

Still, all might have gone well, and Virbena might slowly have returned to

Good, if all the rats hadn't also got out
of the bus and begun to follow them.

It was absolutely to be expected of
course. As far as the poor rats could
see, Virbena was their one chance of
ever being changed back. So when they
saw her disappearing they panicked,
and the only thing they could think of
doing was to stick close to her.

James and Lorna tried to take no
notice of the twitching, twittering mass
following them. They did begin to walk
a little quicker, then even quicker, but
that was no use at all. Rats can run
faster than people if they want.

"James," Lorna panted, behind
their mother's back, "is – she – taking
– us – back – home?"

"I – think – so."

"But – they'll – follow – us – there, –
won't – they?"

"Say – you're – tired – and – you've
– got – to – stop."

"I daren't. You – say."

James didn't dare either. But what
were they going to do when all those
rats crowded into the lift up to their
fourteenth floor flat, and then into the
flat itself? There wasn't room, even if
you actually wanted to share your
home with forty or fifty irritated rats.

Or would Mum not let them in? – in which case they'd be hanging around outside the flat door until she turned Good again.

Virbena was certainly showing no signs of *that*. They passed a couple of lads lounging against a wall, who first blinked, then stared at the procession, till one of them shouted out, "Look at the Pied bloomin' Piper!"

Next moment two more rats were tagging on behind.

A policeman busy telling off a careless parker suddenly turned when he heard the squeals approaching, and moved across to block Virbena's path.

"I must ask you to stop, madam," he said heavily, "because – SQUEAK!!"

And he too tagged on behind.

By the time they began to reach

places that James and Lorna
recognised as near home, Virbena had
added two joggers who'd got in her
way, a small gang of schoolchildren
who'd giggled and an old lady who'd
screamed because she hated rats and
was now probably hating even more
actually being one.

James and Lorna still didn't dare
say anything when Virbena marched,
James and Lorna staggered and the
rest scampered into the entrance to
their block of flats.

There was a lift waiting with its door
open. In swept Virbena, Tuk! went her
finger on the fourteenth floor button.
James and Lorna got in all right, but
the sight of those big lift doors
beginning to slide shut must have
looked awfully threatening from a rat's
point of view, and the ones at the front

made the mistake of hesitating. The last James and Lorna saw of them was their little pink noses pointing in dismay as they saw the doors cutting off their last hope of ever returning to normal.

It was as if Virbena had noticed nothing. When the lift stopped she ushered the children out of it and let them into the flat just as she always did. Then she shut the door and leaned against it, closing her red, smouldering eyes and giving an enormous sigh of relief.

Next moment it was their own dear Good mum standing in front of them.

"Teatime!" she said brightly, as if nothing strange had happened anywhere near her. "What shall we have?" And she began bustling about.

James and Lorna stood looking at

each other in disbelief. It was quite clear that Mum had completely forgotten what she'd left at the lift door. Even now they were sure they could hear rats scampering up and down the stairs outside, searching desperately for Virbena.

It wasn't until tea was on the table and they'd just sat down to eat that either of them dared mention the problem.

"Mum," said James thoughtfully, "you know that witches can turn people into things – well, *you* can, can't you?"

"Yes," said Virbena encouragingly. "What about it?"

"Well, I was just wondering, do they stay turned into the things they've been turned into, or does it sort of wear off?"

"Oh, good Lord, it wears off of course – unless you say something very fancy to fix the spell."

"And do you often do that – say something fancy?" Lorna asked.

"Oh no, I mostly can't be bothered."

"Ah," said James. "So how long would they stay turned if you didn't?"

"Not much more than an hour usually. An hour and a half at most."

James and Lorna smiled happily at each other. Those people would be back to normal any moment now.

Bill Harpy came home for a break from taxi-driving only a few minutes later.

"Can't understand it," he said. "I had to come up the stairs because the lift was full. In fact the whole block's swarming with people I've never seen

58

before, all wandering round asking where they are and how to get out. There was even a policeman and a bus driver on the stairs, asking if this was the right way down. As if they couldn't see which way was down!!"

"How extraordinary!" said Virbena mildly, but it was clear that she wasn't really listening. She seemed more interested in finding out whether Bill wanted to eat his tea now or later.

"It wasn't anything to do with your mumbo-jumbo nonsense, was it?" Bill asked suspiciously.

"Me, dear? How could it be? We've been at the baths all afternoon." You could tell from the surprise on her face that as far as she knew she really was telling the truth.

But Bill still wasn't quite sure. He stared hard at James, then at Lorna.

"Did anything odd happen this afternoon?" he asked them.

"Yeah!" said James. "I swam three strokes without my ring or armbands or anything, and I only put my foot on the bottom once."

"Yes, he did!" said Lorna. "And I jumped in off the side – splash!"

"They'll both be swimming like little frogs soon," Virbena added happily.

As for the other odd thing that had happened, James and Lorna didn't bother to mention that because their father always said he didn't believe in magic. And as for all the people who'd been turned into rats, they didn't know which flat Virbena lived in, and in any case being turned into a rat is not something you'd go round shouting too loudly about, is it?

Chapter 4
The Wizard Barrington

GOOD AND BAD witches like Virbena
are pretty rare. Most witches or
wizards seem to be either mainly good
or mainly bad.

The Wizard Barrington was a bad
one if ever there was. He was someone
Virbena had hated for as long as she
could remember, yet such a
good-looking, smooth-talking wizard
that he seemed like Sportsman and
Disc Jockey of the Year rolled into one.
He thought he was stupendously
wonderful, and so did scores of other
people. Virbena knew him for what he

really was: a cheat, a liar, a scheming sewer-rat.

He had once asked Virbena to marry him, long before she met Bill Harpy. She was very, very beautiful (when she was Good) and the Wizard Barrington didn't believe she could possibly say no to such a wonderful person as he thought she thought he was.

"Marry me, Virbena," he said, "and we will fly broomstick to the South Sea

Isles and make magic under the bright midnight moon."

But Virbena had not only seen through him. She happened to know that he was already married – to a downtrodden, droopy-winged little fairy he kept locked up in a hut in the woods. So she had absolutely no choice about the way she replied. Without wanting to, she went Bad in less than the blink of a bat's eye.

It was the usual performance, smoke and all – but it was a mistake. It meant that Virbena didn't know exactly what she was doing, and the one thing you do have to be sure about if you're going to curse another witch or wizard is that you've planned everything out beforehand. Most spells (though not all) have their anti-spells and counter-spells, and it's so, so easy for the one you're trying to curse to get out from under your spell and lay one on you before you can jump out of cursing range.

In fact dealing with a wizard is quite different from dealing with an ordinary person; it nearly always means a magic-fight.

Fights are nasty to do and boring to describe, so I won't bother you with the huge list of centipedes, skunks, and gobbets of muck, mess and cess that Virbena Harpy and the Wizard Barrington turned each other into that day. In the end they both gave up, exhausted, and walked away from each other, yelling rude words back over their shoulders.

"Snothead!"

"Poo-brain!"

"Spitwit!"

65

And so on, till they were out of wordshot of each other.

Therefore ever since that moment when she had not been able to produce a spell nasty and binding enough to put and keep the Worm Barrington down in the filth where he belonged, Virbena had been walking around with one created specially to deal with him, by her great friend Fay Paradox.

Fay Paradox is so cunning in the ways of magic that there's no magician of any sort who isn't afraid of her power. Yet she's such a sweet-natured person that she'll conjure you a box of Unearthly Delights out of the air if you so much as smile longingly at her.

(Unearthly Delights, by the way, are magic chocolates so delicious that each one tastes as good as a fortnight's holiday on the most exciting beach you could ever dream of.)

To make the spell for her friend
Virbena to lay on the Wizard
Barrington Fay Paradox studied him
for months.

She learned how he wheedled and
charmed his way into the hearts of the
different girls he wanted to marry.

"My word, but you are absolutely one of the most beautiful girls I have ever seen," he would begin, and then he'd go on to tell them what a lonely (but very rich) man he was, and how much he needed a little companion to share his "lonely – but very comfortable – life."

By the time he met Virbena again he had collected about thirty 'wives' in this way, all locked up in various huts in the woods.

Fay Paradox also learned how he lied and flattered his way into the houses of poor old witches and bought from them for a few pence, spells, charms and potions worth thousands of pounds, if they had only known it.

"It's completely worthless – this spell for changing mud into creamy milk chocolate," he would say, "but I'm prepared to give you a couple of pounds for it because I'm feeling in a generous mood today."

When Fay Paradox had finished studying him, she spent days burrowing in old books in the Library of Magic and Mumbo-jumbo, then more days concocting a spell for Virbena, which, because she didn't see the Wizard Barrington for years, Virbena didn't get the chance to use.

Then one day not long ago when she was on her way to Squirmage's for some more supplies, she did suddenly meet him in the street nearby.

She didn't know it was him at first. All she saw was a tall, handsome man in a flashy mauve suit carrying a small suitcase. She saw carefully oiled waves in the hair, sparkling eyes and a

white-toothed smile. Then she began
to recognise him.

He too felt that he recognised
Virbena, but he couldn't think for a
moment who exactly she was. So he
said, "Hello," in his usual charming
way, and politely raised his eyebrows.

It was when he did that, that Virbena
suddenly knew him, and she began to go
Bad immediately, though she just, just
managed to hold it in check while she
rummaged madly in the bottom of her
handbag for the Spell.

She found it in the nick of time. Her

70

hand – almost a green claw already –
grasped that fading, crumbling piece of
paper, pulled it out, opened it, and her
voice that was by now a harsh cackle
began gabbling:

Left foot! Right foot! Fix to the floor.
Not an itchy-bitty twitch for a minute or
more.

(This was to stop him getting away
before she had time to do the rest of
the spell. You have to say the last line
very quickly, which is not easy.)

Truth is the curse I'm laying on you;
The truth you'll tell and the truths you'll
do . . .

(It's no good trying this spell yourself,
by the way, because you have to do
thousands of complicated finger and
nose movements at the same time.)

71

Fraud and falsehood, fibs and fiddles,
Dodgy deals and dirty diddles,
Jiggery-pokery, forgery, flattery;
Lying, spying, treachery, trickery –
Get you gone from this man's mouth,
And leave him naught but simple truth;
The whole truth; nothing but the truth.
Stark-naked, bare, unpainted truth.

(The hardest part of the spell was the bit to stop him from taking it off again the moment she'd gone. For this it is necessary to stand on your head and make complicated *leg* movements. The passers-by did stare rather.)

Spell! Fix well. Fix firm and fast,
Till four and twenty years have passed.

(To do a spell that lasts more than twenty-four years, you have to dance an extremely difficult dance with hundreds of hopsteps, sidesteps and kicksteps. It takes about three hours, and Virbena was not prepared to do that for such trash as the Wizard Barrington.)

When she'd finished, and turned herself right way up, he was just standing looking at her with an amazed sort of glare on his face. Now that the anger was out of her, Virbena was her normal Good and beautiful self again. This time she could remember quite clearly what she'd done when she was Bad, because of having known the spell beforehand.

"It's been most interesting to meet you after all these years," she said politely, beginning to test it out. "And how are all your wives?"

"They are miserable because of the unpleasant way I treat them," the Wizard Barrington answered, equally politely. You could see from the nasty faces he was making that really he wanted to say something different, but couldn't.

"Oh dear," said Virbena, giving a little wriggle of pleasure. "But how about your business? Is that going well?"

"Yes," answered the Wizard Barrington, twisting his mouth all ways about in his efforts to stop it from telling the truth. "I'm still cheating and swindling people a lot, but I haven't got much money because I spend it all on silly things like new silver shoelaces and expensive haircuts."

"How extraordinary," said Virbena. "Well, I must dash. I was just on my way to Squirmage's."

"Ah, so was I," the Wizard Barrington said – then grimacing horribly, "I want to trick him with some rubbishy spells I've made for him to sell."

Virbena was delighted by the spell's success as she followed him into the store. She hung about at the back, pretending to be looking for something

75

very special on the shelves, listening hard.

"Ah, Wizard Barrington, sir," Mr Squirmage said. "And what can I do for you, please? Are you buying or selling today? – and what a lovely day it is."

"I called in because I want to cheat you. No, no, I really meant that – yes, I did. I'm as crooked as a corkscrew, you know."

Mr Squirmage didn't seem to know how to answer. He gave an uneasy laugh, then said, "Well, let's see what you've got for me this week."

The Wizard Barrington lifted his suitcase up onto the counter and threw the lid open. He took out a couple of jars with some evil, black porridgy stuff inside and put them down beside the case.

"I'm very proud of these," he said.

Mr Squirmage looked interested at once.

"And I'm proud of them because – because – that stuff is probably one of the greatest s–s–s–s–"

He stopped with his mouth twisted up in a hideous grin, and Virbena knew that he was desperately trying to say, "spells I've ever made."

What he in fact said was,

"s–s–swindles I've ever tried."

"But does it work?" Mr Squirmage asked (meaning, did it work as a spell?)

"Oh, yes, it works wonderfully," the Wizard Barrington said (meaning that it worked wonderfully as a swindle.) He looked pleased to find that he might still be able to suggest cheaty meanings.

"And what does it do?"

"Ah – hmm – er – it's a – it's supposed to be a cure for baldness." Obviously the Wizard Barrington would have liked to stop there, because a cure for baldness is what all moon-headed men have been seeking for centuries. But Fay Paradox's spell rushed him on to add, "Nothing."

"I beg your pardon, sir?"

"I said 'Nothing'. It does nothing."

81

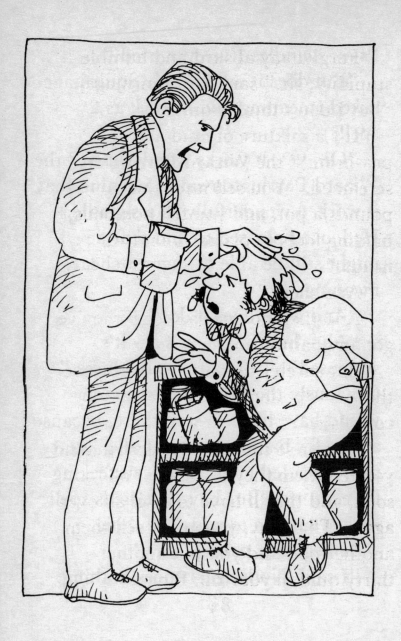

"Forgive my absurd and humble stupidity, sir," said Mr Squirmage, "but I don't think I quite, er . . ."

"It's a mixture of mud and soot, pea-brain!" the Wizard Barrington screamed. "You sell it for thirty pounds a pot, and you tell pompous, balding fools to plaster it on their heads."

"And then?"

"And then no one can see if they've got any hair or not, can they?"

"But surely, sir, when they remove the – er – potion, they come and complain."

"Of course they do, dunderwit. And you tell them they've taken it off too soon, and they'll have to do it all over again. That way, you get to sell them another pot, and you put another thirty quid in your till. Bingo!"

"But when they complain
again . . . ?"

"You tell them the same again! Give
me patience! Don't you see, they've
always taken it off too soon. It's only a
cure for baldness as long as they keep
it plastered on their heads and people
can't see that they're bald!"

"It sounds a little dishonest, sir."

"It isn't a little dishonest, it's a *lot*
dishonest. It's vilely, foully, shockingly
dishonest. It's as dishonest as you are
thick, which is mindboggingly."

Then suddenly the Wizard
Barrington lost patience and gave up.
He plonked the jars back in his case,
slammed and snapped it shut, then
with a wave of his hand and a mutter
he turned Mr Squirmage into a bright
green lizard and swept past Virbena
out of the shop.

Virbena would have stayed to change Mr Squirmage back, only she knew she wouldn't be able to stand his endless creepy 'Thank-yous' if she did, so she slipped out too. She knew it would only take him a few minutes to crawl over to his book of spells and do it for himself anyway.

So that was the end of the Wizard Barrington as a truly bad wizard for a long time. He found himself having to perform honest spells – ones which really worked – for a living, and as he was totally out of practice at doing that he didn't make a very good living. Meanwhile his 'wives' all escaped from their huts in the woods because he couldn't stop himself from taking them to see where the keys were hidden.

Those witches and wizards who'd always known Barrington for what he

86

was were delighted, and they came in a
gang to Virbena's house one afternoon
to congratulate her, while they drank
her lemon tea and ate up all her
chocolate cake.

They had such fun imitating him
telling the truth that they didn't notice
it getting dark outside. But then, since
it *was* dark they all changed themselves
into bats for a giggle and flew off
home.

Hearing the patter-fluttering of so many leathery wings through their bedroom window, James and Lorna looked out just in time to see the dark cloud of bats swoop up and disappear over the trees.

"You know," said Lorna, "it's all right having a mum who's different, really."

"Yes," said James. "And ours is really different!"

Also in Young Puffin

A BAD SPELL FOR THE WORST WITCH

Jill Murphy

A new term spells disaster for Mildred!

Mildred is determined to lose her embarrassing reputation as the worst witch the Academy has ever seen – but things rapidly get out of hand!